W9-AJC-124

DISCARD

MARTY'S MISSION

....· An Apollo 11 Story ·....

Written by Judy Young • Illustrated by David Miles

"Ten, nine, ignition sequence starts," a voice from NASA's Mission Control crackled through the radio.

"Cool!" ten-year-old Marty said to his friend Tomás. "That's what my dad is hearing too!"

"*Five, four, three, two, one, zero,*" Mission Control continued. "*All engines running. Liftoff! Thirty-two minutes past the hour. We have liftoff of Apollo 11.*"

Then a different voice came through the radio.

"Wow!" Tomás said. "That's Armstrong talking from inside the spacecraft!"

"Did you hear how fast it's going?" Marty said. "Over twenty-five thousand feet per second!"

"*Apollo 11 is now orbiting Earth,*" the newscaster on the radio reported. "*In about three hours the Saturn V rocket will put the* Columbia *command module on its pathway to the moon. Four days from now, the lunar module named the* Eagle *will separate from the* Columbia, *taking Neil Armstrong and Buzz Aldrin to the moon's surface. Michael Collins will stay in the* Columbia, *orbiting the moon and waiting for the* Eagle *to return. Then, hopefully, all three astronauts will come safely back to Earth.*"

The newscast ended and Marty turned off the radio.

"Too bad we can't get TV reception," Tomás said as he crawled into bed. "It would have been cool to see it."

"Yeah," Marty agreed, turning off the light. "I wish Dad could have been here, too, but he can't leave the tracking station when there's a spaceflight."

"It's awesome that your dad works for NASA, though," Tomás said.

Apollo 11, the first space mission to put man on the moon, launched just past nine thirty in the morning at Kennedy Space Center. But Guam was fourteen hours ahead of Florida time. It was after eleven thirty at night on the tropical island in the Pacific Ocean. Tomás rolled over and was soon asleep. But Marty lay awake, remembering his visit to the tracking station when his family had first moved to Guam a year ago.

"So this is where I'll work," Dad had said, pulling into a parking lot after an hour's drive through dense tropical forest. "NASA's Guam Tracking Station."

Marty looked around. In a clearing was a large building. Nearby stood a huge antenna, its dish aimed skyward.

"That," Dad said, pointing to the antenna, "is what will pick up communication signals from the spacecraft. And inside the operations building is equipment to relay the signals back and forth between the astronauts and Mission Control in Houston, Texas."

"Will you hear what they say?" Marty asked.

"Every word," Dad said.

"Wow!" Marty exclaimed. "Will you get to watch them too?"

"No, we'll receive TV signals," Dad said, "but we're not set up to televise here, only to relay signals on to Houston."

"Could I come out here when there's a spaceflight?" Marty asked hopefully.

"No," Dad said, "I'll be too busy and there's a lot at stake. If communications go down, the astronauts might not make it home."

Now Marty closed his eyes. He knew he wouldn't see his dad for another eight days. Dad would be busy from blastoff to moon landing to splashdown back on Earth.

Over the next four days, Marty and Tomás were glued to the radio, listening to every update. Finally it was announced that Apollo 11 had entered the moon's orbit. In Guam's time zone, the *Eagle* would land on the moon a little after six the next morning.

The two boys planned to listen together, but late that afternoon Marty got a phone call from his father.

"We've rigged up a TV out here so NASA families can watch the moon landing live," Dad said. "A bus will take everyone to the tracking station."

"All right!" Marty exclaimed. "Can Tomás come too?"

"Sure," Dad said.

Before four the next morning, an excited group crowded around a television at the tracking station. It was tuned to the same news program seen across the ocean on the mainland of the United States. They watched the *Eagle* separate from the *Columbia* and later, with breaths held tight, the group watched the module descend to the lunar surface. A huge cheer roared through the room when Armstrong said, "Houston, Tranquility Base here. The *Eagle* has landed!"

"I can't believe it!" Marty cried. "They're actually sitting on the moon!"

For several hours they watched the *Eagle* on the moon's surface and listened to what the astronauts said inside the lunar module.

"He's coming out!" Marty suddenly exclaimed as a space-suited leg appeared on the ladder under the *Eagle*.

A hush fell over the group as they watched Neil Armstrong take man's first step onto the moon and heard him say, "That's one small step for man, one giant leap for mankind."

For over two hours Armstrong and Aldrin bounced around on the moon, taking photos and collecting lunar rocks. When the astronauts finally went back into the *Eagle*, Marty and the others returned to the bus, talking excitedly about what they had just witnessed.

The next morning, Marty learned that the *Eagle* had left the moon and successfully docked with the *Columbia*. The astronauts would now travel three days back to Earth.

On the last evening of the mission, as Marty crawled into bed, he looked at the crescent-shaped moon shining low in the sky. It somehow seemed different. Apollo 11 would splash down at about three o'clock in the morning, ending the mission, but the US flag and human footprints would still be up on the moon. Thinking about that, Marty shut his eyes and was soon fast asleep.

Suddenly Marty's mom was urgently shaking him. "Wake up!" she said. "Your dad needs you!"

"Needs *me*?" Marty said, sitting up and rubbing his eyes.

"Yes," Mom said. "Someone's here to take you to the tracking station."

"Why?" Marty asked, quickly pulling on his clothes.

"I don't know," Mom said. "Something's gone wrong."

As Marty rode to the tracking station, he worried about what had gone wrong and was puzzled about why his father wanted him.

When he arrived, Dad and several others were waiting near the huge antenna.

"The antenna is stuck," Dad told Marty, "and if we can't get it to move, we can't track Apollo 11. This antenna is the only way Mission Control can communicate with the astronauts from now until splashdown. It's crucial we get it fixed and we don't have much time."

"Why do you need *me*?" Marty asked.

"We think it's a bearing, but we don't have time to take the antenna apart and replace it," Dad said.

"What's a bearing?" Marty asked.

"A ring with metal balls encased inside it, like this." Dad took a bearing from a box and showed it to Marty. "The balls have to roll for the antenna to move, but they're stuck. We hope if we pack the bearing with grease, it will work again. Trouble is, our arms are too big to reach inside. Do you think you can do it?"

"You bet!" Marty exclaimed.

After listening to Dad's instructions, Marty climbed the stairs below the huge antenna dish, carrying a big pail of grease. He squeezed into the tight inner area that housed the motor. With a glob of grease in his hand, Marty tried to stick his arm into the narrow hole where the bearing was, but even his arm was too big.

Marty looked up at the sky. Somewhere in that black expanse of space were three astronauts whose lives depended on this antenna to help land them safely back on Earth.

I have to find a way, Marty thought. He looked at the grease in his hand and then smiled.

Quickly, Marty smeared grease all over his arm. Then, grabbing another glob, he shoved his arm back into the hole. It was tight, but the grease helped his arm slip in. Marty crammed the handful of grease around the bearing. Over and over, he packed in more grease until the pail was empty. Then he backed out and raced down the stairs.

"Give it a try," Dad called out toward the operations building.

Everyone held their breath, looking up at the huge antenna. It seemed like forever, but it finally creaked and slowly started moving. Instantly a voice called out from the building. "Communications with Apollo 11 intact. All systems working!"

"Way to go!" the men cheered, slapping Marty on the back and congratulating him. "You did it! How's it feel to be part of the Apollo 11 mission?"

"Great!" Marty exclaimed, his face beaming under smears of grease.

Inside the operations building, Marty sat next to his father, listening as the spacecraft returned to Earth's atmosphere. Then suddenly he heard cheering and applause from Houston as a voice said, *"Successful splashdown—task accomplished! Welcome back to Earth, Apollo 11."*

Everyone at the tracking station cheered, too. Then Dad wrapped his arm around Marty's shoulders and, squeezing him tight, said, "The world wouldn't have heard those words if it weren't for you, son."

···· AUTHOR'S NOTE ····

BY 1961, THE UNITED STATES had been in a space race with the Soviet Union (USSR) for four years. And the Soviets had had many firsts—first to orbit Earth, first animal to orbit Earth, first to leave Earth's orbit, first to make physical contact with the moon, and first to put a man in space. The United States was lagging behind in second place. On May 25, President John F. Kennedy set a lofty goal: The United States would commit itself to "landing a man on the moon and returning him safely to Earth" by the end of the decade. The space race heated up and the prize hung in the sky for all the world to see—the moon.

Over 400,000 people put their hearts and souls into the project—from the engineers who designed rocket motors and spacecraft, to the mechanics who built them, to the seamstresses who sewed space suits, and all the way to the janitors who swept the floors. One individual was ten-year-old Greg Force, who was brought to a tracking station on the US territory of Guam to grease a failed bearing on an antenna in the final hours of the Apollo 11 mission. *Marty's Mission* is a fictitious story based on that real event.

On July 20, 1969, the whole world watched as the first person, an American, took the first step on the moon. I was thirteen years old, and my family and I were on vacation in Gatlinburg, Tennessee. Television sets were everywhere: in store windows, on restaurant counters, in gas stations. Crowds gathered around watching, waiting, with everyone holding their breath as the *Eagle* landed on the moon. Late that evening in our motel room, my family and I watched man's first step on the lunar surface. Little did I know then that a half century later, my son would be one of a team of aerospace engineers working toward another giant leap for mankind—putting man on Mars.

For Tucker—
Look toward the moon and dream!

Love,
Grandma

For my boy, Zane!
You don't have to be a grown-up
to reach for the stars!

—David

Text Copyright © 2019 Judy Young • Illustration Copyright © 2019 David Miles • Design Copyright © 2019 Sleeping Bear Press

Printed and bound in the United States.

10 9 8 7 6 5 4 3 2 1

Library of Congress Cataloging-in-Publication Data

Names: Young, Judy, 1956- author. | Miles, David, 1973- illustrator. Title: Marty's mission : an Apollo 11 story / written by Judy Young ; illustrated by David Miles. Other titles: Tales of young Americans series. Description: Ann Arbor, MI : Sleeping Bear Press, [2019] | Series: The tales of young Americans | Summary: As the Apollo 11 mission draws to a close there is a crisis at the tracking station on Guam: the antenna that will track the spacecraft during reentry, and allow mission control to communicate with the astronauts is stuck—and ten-year-old Marty is the only one small enough to reach in and grease the ball bearings that allow the antenna to move. Identifiers: LCCN 2018037160 | ISBN 9781534110144 (hardcover) | Subjects: LCSH: Apollo 11 (Spacecraft)—Juvenile fiction. | Project Apollo (U.S.)—Juvenile fiction. | Tracking (Engineering)—Juvenile fiction. | Radar—Antennas—Juvenile fiction. | CYAC: Apollo 11 (Spacecraft)—Fiction. | Project Apollo (U.S.)—Fiction. | Space flight to the moon—Fiction. Classification: LCC PZ7.Y8664 Mar 2019 | DDC 813.6 [Fic] —dc23 | LC record available at https://lccn.loc.gov/2018037160